THE CHRONICLES OF CYPURIC

BOOK 1: A LEADER HAS RISEN

E. R. Johnson

Words Matter Publishing

P.O. Box 531

Salem, Il 62881

www.wordsmatterpublishing.com

ISBN 13: 978-1-947072-72-5

ISBN 10: 1-947072-72-2

Library of Congress Catalog Card Number: 2018943420

PROLOGUE

The chilling silence enveloped the two Crystal Ice dragons that stood in the center of the cavern. Thick ice walls stretched over their heads, ending in a sharp point above them.

Multa, the older of the two dragons, shivered and beat her wings nervously. "Are you sure about this, Agor?" Her voice was barely above a soft whisper, and her breath made small clouds in the chilled air.

"Yes. I am sure." Agor turned to face an egg that sat glittering upon a snow-white marble pedestal. "It is our only hope for survival."

Multa frowned and looked away from Agor so he wouldn't see the uncertainty in her eyes. Usually, she respected the young leader's decisions, but this time his idea made her think twice.

Then the sound of claws scraping on ice echoed throughout the mountain, sending chills up Multa's spine. It could only mean one thing: *Kios was coming.*

"Oh, no." Multa backed away from the sealed mouth of the

cave. "He is here!"

The hastily made sheet of ice covering the cavern entrance shattered, scattering shards of ice. Standing in the once-concealed doorway was a dragon. His jagged green-black scales shrouded him in darkness; his razor-sharp claws embedded themselves in the fragile ice floor with a painful grating noise.

"Kios." Agor spat the name out like poison.

Kios's purple eyes flashed angrily. He yanked his claws free from the ice and viciously swiped at Agor's wings. Agor nimbly dodged the attack and countered with one of his own, slashing Kios across the chest with equally sharp claws.

Kios looked down and saw murky silver blood pooling at his feet. "You will pay for that, you golden-blooded oaf!" He lunged towards Agor.

Locked in a violent battle, the two dragons rolled into walls and the gleaming pedestal. The egg teetered precariously, and Kios stretched his lips into a gruesome grin.

"Multa!" Agor roared, momentarily distracted from his fight, "go warn the others!"

Kios clawed Agor across his eye. "Not so strong now, are you?" he taunted.

Agor howled in pain, his right eye already swelling from Kios's dark poison.

"Agor!" Multa leaped forward, but she was too late.

Kios gouged Agor directly through the stomach, an unhidden look of glee in his eyes. He turned to Multa. "Your turn next," he sneered.

Multa dodged Kios's hulking form and flew out of the cavern, leaving the mountain behind, bearing the news of Agor's death with a heavy heart.

Kios kicked Agor's body aside. "Glad that's over. Now for that wretched egg."

The crystalline egg seemed to already know of its fate, for it flew off of the pedestal and smashed through the icy cavern wall into the raging battle outside.

"NO!" Kios swept his bloodied claws through the pedestal, and the marble crumbled to dust.

"Kirvam, my daughter," Agor whispered, golden blood dripping from his wounds, "you have made it."

Those were his final words.

The sixth graders of Mr. Venegas's class at Nikola Tesla Elementary School stared at the classroom clock, impatiently waiting for the bell to ring. This bell would signal the arrival of 12:30 p.m., the time of recess. Each pair of feet shuffled under each of the desks, ignoring Mr. Venegas rattle on about onomatopoeias and alliteration. Kira Nielson, one such sixth grader, also glanced up at the classroom clock then back to her digital watch. She brushed her jet-black hair out of her face, wondering if the two clocks were in sync. Both her watch and the classroom clock ticked off the seconds, and each student muttered the countdown.

Then the sharp, piercing sound of the dismissal bell rang throughout the entire school, sending grades one through six out to the playground.

Kira was one of the first students to bolt out the classroom door. She grabbed her jacket from her locker and ran towards the exit.

"Hey, Kira!" a voice called from behind her.

Kira turned around and saw that it was her best friend Luke Owens, an athletic fifth grader with short brown hair and freckles from Ms. Nicoletta's class. Standing beside him was another one of her friends, Neeley.

"Yeah?" Kira knelt down and tied the laces of her Skechers.

Luke bounced a rubber kickball on the tiled hall floor. "Want to play soccer with us at recess?"

"Sure!" Kira walked towards the north exit with Luke and Neeley. They laughed and chatted down the hall, making jokes and telling stories about their days. Suddenly, Kira saw a large, red bird crash down from the sky.

"Guys, I just saw a bird fall out of the sky!" Kira rushed outdoors and onto the playground, with her friends right behind. She whipped her head around, scanning the jungle gym. Then the blacktop, and then the field, looking for the mysterious bird. Then she spotted a flash of red beneath an aspen tree. "Gotcha," she murmured, beelining towards the object.

The bird appeared strange up close. Kira knelt down and gazed upon it. It was like a large bird, but it had four legs, shimmery red scales, and two scarlet wings folded on its sides. One wing was bent at an odd angle, and the creature was breathing heavily, sending little puffs of smoke out her nostrils. Golden blood leaked from a wound in her side.

Kira opened her mouth to speak, but instead, she heard the creature speak.

My name is Edeerna. The creature spoke in a strange, fluty language, and her voice was weak.

What are you? Kira was surprised to hear herself reply in the language she had never learned.

A dragon of Fire.

Kira stopped, too confused to ask another question. She definitely had to be hallucinating. Dragons didn't exist!

Kirvam…

My name is Kira.

Kirvam…Kios is coming!

"Kira!" Neeley said, running towards Kira, "you okay?"

The bluntness of the English language snapped Kira out of her private conversation with the dragon. "Of course not! This weird bird—dragon—just started speaking to me!"

Neeley gave Kira a weird look. "Kira, there's nothing there."

"Don't you see the *dragon?*" Kira's breath caught in her throat.

Luke ran up to the two girls. "What's wrong?"

"Luke, go get Mr. Rogers, please."

Luke gave Kira a worried glance before jogging back to the school building.

All of a sudden Kira lurched forward and retched as bile rose up in her throat. Something dark was nearby, and she could sense it.

"Kira Nielson, you shouldn't be at school like this!" a voice commanded haughtily.

Kira looked up into the stern eyes of Vice Principal Rogers. "Ugh," was all she could groan in reply, falling to her knees.

"Neeley, please go tell the front office to call Mrs. Nielson at once. Tell her that Kira has fainted," Mr. Rogers ordered. As soon as Neeley was gone, he leaned down and stared at Kira square in the eye. "Remember: you saw nothing." His eyes flashed blood-red, then he turned his back to Kira, facing the dragon. She saw his fist rise up and she thought she heard a cry of pain.

"*Edeerna,*" Kira tried to say, but the ground swayed towards her, and the world went dark.

Kira slowly opened her eyes and groaned. "What happened?" she said to her empty bedroom. Then the memories came back. Edeerna, Mr. Rogers's blood-red eyes, her blackout. And those menacing words he spoke: *"You saw nothing."*

Kira threw off her sheet and jumped out of bed. "Mom?" she called tentatively down the upstairs hall.

"I'm downstairs, sweetie," her mother called back.

Kira ran down the stairs and slid into a seat at the kitchen breakfast nook. Michaela Nielson, Kira's mother, set a plate with a sandwich on it down in front of her. "Eat up, Kira. I don't want you to black out again."

Kira wolfed down the ham and cheese sandwich and took a long drink of milk. "What happened?"

Her mother sat down across from her and sighed. "I was so worried, Kira. The vice principal called—"

"Mr. Rogers?"

"Yes. Well, he called and said that you had a heat stroke. He asked me to come pick you up right away."

Kira paused with her milk glass inches from her mouth. "That's not what happened."

Her mother arched an eyebrow. "Really?"

"Yeah. I was about to go outside for recess when I saw a bird fall out of the sky. I went to go look at it, but it was a dragon, and nobody else could see it!"

Her mother gave her a sympathetic smile. "Mr. Rogers said you had been mumbling about dragons and something called Edeerna. He said hallucinations were a sure sign of heat stroke."

Kira slammed her glass down on the table, sending milk sloshing out of it. "Why does nobody believe me?"

"Sweetie, why don't you go rest for now. You can take tomorrow off from school, too."

Kira huffed and clattered her dishes into the sink. "I'll be upstairs."

She stormed down the hall, up the stairs, and slammed her bedroom door shut. With a heavy sigh, Kira closed her eyes and slept. She dreamt of Edeerna, the small dragon, and Mr. Rogers with blood-red eyes.

—

"Ki-ra! Time for dinner!"

Kira jumped up, startled. She blinked and remembered where she was. "Coming!"

She ran downstairs to the kitchen and grabbed a plate. "What's for dinner?" she asked.

Her mother scooped a spoonful of cheesy pasta onto Kira's plate. "Bite-sized cheese lasagna."

Kira smiled. "My favorite!"

Her mother returned the smile

Then Kira jumped off the couch, pulled on her sneakers, and bolted outside. Fresh air flooded her lungs, and it seemed as if all of the darkness was swept away. "I'm going to the Woods, Mom!"

"Kira, wait right there!" her mother yelled.

Kira ignored her and kept running to the Woods.

The Woods wasn't really a forest; it was more of a thicket of evergreens with a small circle of grass in the center. Once she was in the Woods, Kira laid down upon the cool grass and took deep breaths of the crisp air. Blades of grass swayed gently in the breeze, and the trees danced, scattering the sharp, bitter scent of pine. "It's beautiful," Kira whispered in awe, gazing upward at a flock of songbirds soaring through the blue sky.

"I know. It really makes you wonder why those idiotic humans are killing every blooming thing in sight," came a casual voice from Kira's right.

"What?" Kira cried, whirling around to take a look at the speaker. It was a boy, a boy wearing a blue suit that looked like a cross between a wetsuit and a spacesuit. He was hovering mere inches above the ground, the white-hot flames issuing from his boots barely scorching the green grass.

"Crazy, huh?" the boy continued, running his hand through his spiky black hair.

"Get away from me!" Kira clambered to her feet, trying to get away from this strange boy, but he grabbed her wrist and rocketed into the sky. "Help! Mom, HELP!" Kira screamed until her throat was sore.

"Kira! No! I'm not ready!" Mrs. Nielson leaped up from where she was sitting and snatched at Kira, only to find she was clutching empty air.

"Mom! Do something!" Kira's hand stretched out to her mother, fingers spread wide. As she watched her home get farther and farther away, Kira attempted to kick the curious boy.

"OW! What the heck?" he exclaimed, quite literally dropping Kira like a hot potato.

Kira screamed as the ground grew closer to her face. She flew past oaks, aspens, and firs. Branches scratched her arms and face as she reached out and grabbed an overhanging limb of a pine. The sudden lunge jarred Kira's shoulder, and she grimaced as her palms scraped against the rough bark. Kira gently loosened her grip on the branch and carefully dropped down into soft foliage. She took a step back, then stopped as she heard pebbles falling down the chasm below.

"Oh, no," Kira whispered.

She turned around and found herself on the edge of a sheer cliff and face to face with Mr. Rogers! His eyes widened in surprise, and he backed away from Kira. "Wha-? No! It can't be!"

Rogers cried. When he realized that she wasn't going to move, his eyes narrowed angrily and turned blood-red. "Get out of my way, brat!" he snarled.

Kira did the exact opposite of what he expected. She planted her feet firmly on the ground and kicked Rogers in the shins. He keeled over, scrabbling for a handhold with desperate fingers as he slid down the mountainside. Kira closed her eyes and covered her ears so she wouldn't hear his pained cry "Oh. My. Gosh." Kira whispered. "I think I just killed Mr. Rogers!".

Suddenly Rogers flew up from the jagged rocks below, great leathery wings protruding from his back. Kira screamed as his canines transformed into inhuman fangs. He swooped towards her, teeth bared, and Kira curled into a ball.

When nothing happened for quite a long time, Kira opened her eyes and saw the boy again, but this time he was holding Rogers around the neck. Rogers's face was turning dark purple, and he was beginning to struggle, his sharp inhuman nails clawing at the boy's fingers. The boy sighed like he'd seen this before and stuck a dagger into Roger's stomach and dropped him onto the rocks. He and Kira stood absolutely still until Rogers's low, guttural cry echoed around them.

"Hey, Kirvam!" the boy cried, landing beside Kira. "Are you ready?"

Kira screamed and backed right into another boy, this one wearing a T-shirt that read "COOL," blue jeans, and sunglasses. His nose looked like it had been broken, his brown eyes were laughing, and light facial hair dotted his upper lip and chin. Kira screamed yet again. "What was that thing?"

"Oh, just a shape-shifting dragon," spaceboy said airily.

"A what?"

"A dragon that can shape-shift into anything, the only giveaway being their blood-red eyes."

Kira looked down the chasm at Rogers's mangled corpse. "Why was it my vice principal?"

The new boy shrugged. "Probably just a cover. His real name, his dragon name, was Riklow."

Kira shuddered. "Who are you, people?"

"We're the guys—" began spaceboy.

"Who save lives!" new boy chortled.

They looked at each other like the center of the universe had just been discovered.

"Hey," spaceboy whispered, "that rhymed!"

Then they fell on top of each other, laughing so hard that tears came to their eyes. Kira put her hands on her hips, trying to maintain her cool. "I meant who you *really* are," she said coolly.

Spaceboy wiped his eyes. "Sorry 'bout that." He stuck out his hand for Kira to shake, but she looked at the hand like it was a gigantic scorpion. "Uh, I'm Zero."

The other boy elbowed Zero. "*This* is Zero Georges, and I'm Kyle Delaney."

"Well then, Zero Georges and Kyle Delaney," Kira continued, "I have some more questions for you."

"They'll all be answered as soon as we get to Cypuric, Kirvam,"

Zero assured Kira.

"Wait—what's Cypuric?" Kira asked.

"Your home," Kyle said matter-of-factly. "Let's get to the portal now."

Zero grabbed Kyle and Kira by the wrist and rocketed into the sky. "Where are we going?" questioned Kira nervously.

Kyle pointed to a swirling mass of color that was getting larger by the minute. "There!" he shouted.

"Is that…?" Kira said weakly.

"A portal!" Zero cried over his shoulder.

Kira struggled against Zero's iron grip, but it was too late. They were thrust violently into the portal, and Kira felt like she was in a giant clothes dryer. Then all sense of time was lost to Kira, and she closed her eyes, succumbing to the hypnotic movement of color.

"Not bad for a first try," Zero commented.

"Second," corrected Kyle.

"Right."

"What're you guys blabbering about?" Kira snapped. She felt like she had just stepped off of the Cannibal rollercoaster at Lagoon. Everything was spinning, and she wanted to puke.

Kyle winked. "Nothing, really."

Kira stood up straight. "Take me home right now!"

Introductions first," Zero said briskly.

Kira rolled her eyes. "We already had those!"

Zero decided to ignore her. "I'm Zero, this is Kyle, and we're—"

"A couple of psychopathic kidnappers," Kira spat. "NOW TAKE ME HOME."

Kyle shrugged. "No can do, Kirvam."

"WHY N-wait, why did you call me Kirvam?"

"'Cause that's your name, girlfriend!" Kyle crowed. Zero shot him a look that clearly read death, and they immediately began to bicker like a group of toddlers over a toy.

Kira closed her mouth and turned her attention to the scenery around her. Tall pine trees cut through the sky like jagged knives, the marshy ground seeped muddy water, and a swirling fog enveloped them. "Where are we?"

Zero stopped fighting and looked around. "Oh, no," he muttered, "Mist dragon territory."

"Um, is that bad?" Kira questioned nervously.

Kyle nodded vigorously. "They're-OUCH!" he yelped as a jet of hazy fire blasted his back.

Zero jumped in front of the other two and shot beams of pure light at the Mist dragons, causing them to scream in pain and momentarily retreat. Kyle clambered to his feet and prepared to join the battle, but then a hazel-eyed girl with caramel hair leaped from the treetops and slipped a pair of lethal-looking daggers from her belt. "I can't believe I'm always picking up after you guys!" she groaned good-naturedly. The daggers she held burst into flames, the girl flicked her wrists, and they sliced through all of the dragons before returning boomerang-style to her ready hands.

"We had everything under control, Cierra," Zero seethed.

Cierra laughed. "Of course you did."

Suddenly a not quite defeated Mist dragon shot fine ice particles at Cierra's chest, slamming her into a nearby tree.

"Cierra!" Zero cried. He blushed. "Uh, I mean, are you okay?"

"Yep! All good!" Cierra cried, leaping to her feet. "Boulder silk saves lives," she added, pointing to her shimmery rainbow shirt, "you guys should really wear yours."

"In your dreams," Zero grumbled.

"*Now* can I go home?" Kira pleaded. "And who are you?"

Cierra gave her a funny look. "I'm Cierra Thompson, and you *are* home, Kirvam. You're in Cypuric, your birthplace."

Kirvam backed away. "I think you've made a mistake. I'm not a dragon. I'm a sixth grader who lives in Utah, for Pete's sake!"

"They haven't told you, then," Cierra stated glumly.

"Who's 'they'?"

"Your parents," Cierra replied.

"My…parents?" Kirvam asked. She was so confused.

"Yes." Zero sighed. "But bear with me: Alec will explain everything as soon as we get there."

Kirvam slowly sat down. "Okay," she whispered hoarsely.

"Alrighty then," said Kyle, helping Kirvam to her feet, "according to my map, there are only about two miles left until we get to the kingdom of Alatrusa. That means we should be there in an hour."

Unfortunately, the trip took three hours because there was actually five miles left. Tired and hungry, the determined foursome stopped at the base of a tall mountain that stood in the center of many small mounts. The mountain was a lot taller than a football goalpost, reaching way into the sky. Frigid winds swirled around them, chilling everyone to the bone. Cierra stood in front of the others, placing her right hand on the mountain's icy surface wherever she could reach, in hopes of unlocking some secret entrance.

"Hurry up already!" Zero complained, growing impatient of watching Cierra's struggles.

"News flash, Zero, I can't do everything in five seconds just 'cause I'm your crush," Cierra snapped.

Zero turned tomato red and swore under his breath.

Then a chunk of ice slid neatly away, leaving a gaping, pitch-black hole that led into a large cavern. The cavern was cold and spacious and in the middle of it stood an ornate granite pedestal. Next to the pedestal was a boy with bristly brown hair, worried milk chocolate eyes, and rumpled clothes.

Cierra stepped forward, and the ice covered the entrance again. "Alec, we're here," she said, and the boy looked up from his work.

"Hello Cierra, Kyle, Zero-who are you?"

"It's her, Alec!" Zero cried, exasperated.

"Who?" Alec replied, a clearly confused look on his face.

"*HER!*" shrieked Zero.

"Oh yeah, Kirvam," Alec said distantly.

Zero rolled his eyes. "Duh!"

"So, how'd it go?" asked Alec.

"Well, we had to stop Riklow back on Earth," Kyle began.

"Yeah, then I had to save their *be*-hinds from a *buttload* of Mist dragons!" Cierra added.

Alec nodded. "Good to know."

"Excuse me, Alec?" Kirvam said tentatively.

"Yes?" Alec turned from the pedestal.

"Can you tell me what's going on?"

"Certainly," he replied, "but it may take a while."

CHAPTER FOUR

"First," Kira said, "I want to know what those Mist dragon thingies are."

Cierra waved her hand. "Oh, those are just dragons who essentially got 'killed,' and now they're shells of their former selves."

Kira shuddered. "That's dark."

Alec cleared his throat.

"Sorry," Cierra said sarcastically, "it's Alec's turn to be in the limelight.

"It all started a long time ago, back when the dragons lived peacefully alongside humans," Alec began, gesturing with his hands to tell the action of the story.

"Puh-lease skip the boring history crap and get to the good part!" Zero grumbled.

"Yeah!" agreed Kyle. "You could hardly call their relationship peaceful. There were bajillions of bloody battles during that era!"

"Shut up," Alec growled through clenched teeth. "I'm *trying* to tell a story here."

"Sorry," Zero and Kyle whispered meekly.

"As I was saying, the dragons and humans lived *almost* peaceful-ly-ya happy?-until the humans declared war on the dragons."

"Wait," Kirvam interrupted, "you're saying we're the bad guys. Are we the bad guys?"

Alec sighed. "Not anymore. Anyway, centuries later Nikolai Raylos founded the Dragon Keepers, an organization dedicated to protecting the dragons. And just a mere twelve years ago, you, Kirvam, were born. Unfortunately, a ruthless tyrant was bent on ruling all of Cypuric. He stormed throughout the land with the Ragnauts, his hand-picked army that is dedicated to killing, slaughtering any dragon or human that stood in his way.

"Thankfully, your father made the decision to send you to Earth, only to return when Cypuric was in dire need. Other dragons did this too, though not all of the attempts were successful."

Kirvam nodded, though she was still more than a little confused. "Kay, I'm supposed to save Cypuric, but I still don't know who or what I am."

"You are Kirvam the First Leader, daughter of Agor, who was the leader of the Crystal Ice dragons," Alec explained.

"What do you mean by 'was'?" Kirvam asked suspiciously.

Alec sighed again. "Agor met an untimely death when he battled for your life against Kios."

"Kios…" Kirvam furrowed her brow in concentration. "I've heard that name before… Oh yeah!" Kirvam snapped her fingers. "A dragon named Edeerna landed at my school and told me Kios was coming!"

Alec, Cierra, Kyle, and Zero's faces went white with fear. "Oh, no, this is bad, this is very, very bad," Alec muttered nervously.

"What's bad?" questioned Kirvam.

"Kios is coming, and he's going to kill us all!" Zero screeched. "Man, for being the new leader you're surprisingly stupid."

"Zero! Don't!" hissed Kyle after whacking Zero upside the head.

"Ow!" Zero whined.

"To put Zero's message more eloquently, Edeerna was a dragon spy of ours who was sent to the Ragnauts' lair to pinpoint the next attack location," Alec said.

"Okay, Kios is going to kill us, but how am I a dragon?" asked Kirvam.

"We'll get to that," Alec said vaguely.

"And who's Kios?" Kirvam added.

"Kios is the blackest-hearted, most silver-blooded Krump dragon I have ever met!" Zero spat.

"Silver blooded?" questioned Kirvam.

"It's a dragon term," Kyle offered. "It means you're a tyrant or something."

Kirvam summed up everything she had learned and asked her final question. "Who are you guys?"

"Us?" clarified Kyle.

"We are the Dragon Keepers," Alec said grimly, "we are the last hope for all."

CHAPTER FIVE

"Our first step is to find Multa," instructed Alec, pushing a button on the granite pedestal.

About five seconds later a hologram appeared on the pedestal. "Wow," breathed Kirvam. She was looking at a map of Cypuric, laid out entirely in holographic miniature. Virtual mountains, rivers, lakes, and streams dotted the computer-generated landscape.

"This," Alec said with a flourish, "is our key to defeating Kios."

Cierra, however, didn't wait for fancy introductions. She stepped up to the pedestal and commanded the computer to show her Multa. The original hologram fizzled out, only to be replaced with a zoomed-in picture of a cluster of caves. "Got it! She's in the Phenox Dragon Caves!" Cierra slammed her hand on the top of the pedestal, sending a small avalanche of granite pebbles showering down. Alec gave her a withering look. "Sorry," she said sheepishly.

"Okay, if we have to be there, let's get going!" Kyle cried.

"Yeah," Zero agreed, "the sooner Kirvam's in dragon form the better."

The Dragon Keepers exited the cavern and began their long trek to Multa's cave. After plenty of struggling to find footing on the icy ground, they arrived in a new kingdom.

"Garalon," Kyle whispered. The name had an ominous air to it, and it hung in the air like a cloud of misfortune.

Kirvam had no clue why the rest of the Dragon Keepers kept darting around nervously and ducking behind boulders and trees. Garalon looked very beautiful and lush to her, especially compared to icy Alatrusa, which always seemed to be in some sort of blizzard.

"Here we are!" Alec exclaimed gaily. He pointed to a small cave that was about a quarter of a mile away. "You're the only one who's supposed to enter, Kirvam."

Kirvam took a deep breath. Slowly but carefully she walked into the wide mouth of the cave. Inside of the small space was a large, round stone with a dragon perched upon it. "M-multa?" Kirvam stuttered.

The dragon looked up, and Kirvam realized that its eyes were clouded and blind, its scales resembling a tarnished mirror. "Who are you?" she croaked.

"I am Kirvam, daughter of Agor."

Multa stood up and began to recite a peculiar chant.

> "Rethguad fo Roga,
> Ekat ym dnah.
> Uoy era ya nogard,
> Ni yna dnal."

"What does it mean?" Kirvam whispered, though the words, in English, were coming to her."

"Say it in your language."

> "Daughter of Agor,
> Take my hand.

You are a dragon,
In any land."

Kirvam looked down at her hand. Nestled in her palm was a smooth, hexagonal crystal striped with turquoise and pale blue. "What is it?" asked Kirvam, holding the crystal up to the light.

"An activator stone," Multa said simply as if that explained everything.

"A wha-?" Kirvam stopped talking as the stone began to vibrate. The crystal stripes rippled, and a freezing sensation spread throughout her body. It felt as if frigid water was dripping from every pore.

"You can open your eyes now," Multa said gently.

Kirvam opened her eyes and looked at herself. Claws protruded from her feet, her scales shimmered and danced in the dim light, and her senses were sharper than ever. "I'm… a dragon."

"Yes. And it is time to stop Kios."

Halfway to the exit Kirvam stopped and turned around. "Multa, do you ever miss… you know, seeing?"

"Child, I am old, and my eyes have seen enough," Multa said. "It is now your turn to see new things."

"Thank you." Kirvam faced forward and quickly walked away.

"So, how'd it go?" Zero asked casually.

"It obviously went well," Cierra said before Kirvam could answer, "I mean, c'mon, Zero, how dumb can you be? She's in dragon form, after all."

"I was *trying* to start a conversation," Zero grumbled.

"Let's get back to Alatrusa, guys," Alec said, "we better hurry if we don't want to die today."

As they left Multa and started to return to their own cavern, Kirvam studied her new reflection in small puddles and pondered Alec's words: Would they really die today?

CHAPTER SIX

"First things first," said Zero, his mental gears already turning, "we need to form an army."

Kyle rolled his eyes. "Seriously? Buddy, you planned way too far ahead."

This time it was Zero's turn to whack Kyle, and, before long, the two were locked in a close-to-eternal battle of vulgar language.

"Guys! Guys! Cut it out! I said, CUT IT OUT!" Alec roared after several attempts to end the small war.

Kyle and Zero stopped bickering, but they still kept giving each other I'm-gonna-kill-you-in your-sleep glares.

Kirvam cleared her throat. "I think we should listen to Zero."

Zero threw his arms up. "Finally!"

"Anyway," Kirvam continued, giving Zero an annoyed look, "there's no way five twelve-year-olds can defeat Kios."

"Hey! I'm fifteen!" Kyle said defiantly.

"Yeah and I'm fourteen!" Zero added.

"What Kirvam's trying to say is that we're weak," Cierra said, "but we're not. We've been preparing for this fight all of our lives, and I think we're ready. All in favor say 'aye.'"

"Aye," said Alec.

"Me too!" Kyle cried. "I mean aye!"

"Aye," Kirvam whispered.

They all looked expectantly at Zero. "Fine!" he griped, "but you're gonna get us all killed."

After a moment of silence, Kirvam spoke again. "Cierra, you said that my parents were supposed to tell me something, but they didn't. What was it?"

Cierra shook her head. "They were supposed to explain your past."

"Why didn't they?"

"They were going to… when you were eighteen. We needed you *now*, so we resorted to—"

"Kidnapping?' Kirvam interrupted.

"Kirvam, it's not like that," Cierra began.

"Yes, it is!"

"Let's just go." Alec faced forward and began to walk.

Soon the Dragon Keepers arrived back at their icy mountain base. Kirvam paused every few yards or so, stopping to marvel at the awesome ice structure that surrounded them.

"Come on," Cierra beckoned.

Alec led the group up a spiral staircase made of gray stone and through an oak door. They stepped into a corridor with three doors on both sides.

"Cierra, Kir, you're in there," Kyle said, nodding his head at the first door on the left. "We're across from you; your bathroom's next door."

Cierra pushed open the door, and the two girls stepped inside. Their room was simply furnished: wooden panels on the floors and walls, two cots with wool blankets on either side of the room, and a chest of drawers with a couple of flashlights on top of it. Kirvam turned into a human and sat down on the bed. "Are there any clothes for me to wear?" she asked.

Cierra knelt down on the wood floor and yanked open the dresser drawers. "Um, there's a boulder silk tunic, some T-shirts, socks, jeans, and underwear."

"I'll use all of 'em, thanks," said Kirvam, "but what's so special about boulder silk?"

"Are you kidding?" Cierra cried. "Just look at my shirt. Boulder silk is invincible, sewn by dragons of long ago on a stone loom. It's how my spine didn't break when I was fighting the Mist dragons."

"Oh." Kirvam slipped the tunic over her head and kicked off her shoes. "Well, g'night then."

"G'night," Cierra replied sleepily. "Try not to get yourself killed tomorrow."

Kirvam turned over in her bed and closed her eyes, dreaming of a menacing dragon that spat fire at her. *"Don't give him your eyes, child,"* Multa said, *"you are too young."*

"Rise and shine!"

Kirvam opened her eyes and saw Cierra sitting across from her, tying her pair of sneakers tightly. "Morning," Kirvam replied, sitting up in bed.

"There's your breakfast," Cierra said, nodding at the cheese bagel, apple, and glass of water that sat on the nightstand.

After stuffing the bagel into her mouth and gulping down the water, Kirvam pulled on her Converse and followed Cierra back to the central room. On the way out she grabbed the apple and shoved it into her jeans pocket for later. In the main room, a man stood at the pedestal, gazing intently at the hologram on it. He had dark hair, wrinkled clothes, and looked as if he hadn't shaved in days.

"Alec, I think I know where Kios is," he said, barely lifting his bloodshot eyes to look at the girls.

"Hey, Kevin," Cierra said, joining him by the pedestal. "Kirvam, this is Kevin. Kevin, meet Kirvam."

"Hello, Kirvam." Kevin extended his hand, and Kirvam shook it. "I'm Alec's uncle."

"Hi," Kirvam said in reply.

Alec stepped into the room, along with Zero and Kyle. "What'd I miss?" Zero asked.

"Good morning Alec, Kyle, Zero," said Kevin. "I think I know where Kios's lair is."

"Great!" cried Alec. "Where?"

"The Forever Mountains, in Garalon."

"What are we waiting for, then?" Kirvam asked.

"Yeah!" added Zero. "Let's go kick some dragon butt!"

Cierra and Kyle rolled their eyes. "Guys, we need to formulate a plan first," Alec explained.

"So, no sneak attacks," Zero sighed wistfully.

"Sadly, no," said Kevin. "It may seem pretty easy, but there's no telling what horrific methods Kios is using to guard his lair. We need to stay on our toes."

"'Kay," Alec said, "Kevin, Zero, Kyle, and I will strategize on entrance plans. Cierra, take a look at the Dragon Guide for any tips on Krump dragon ways of defending."

"What about me?" questioned Kirvam.

"Ah, just join any group," said Alec.

Kirvam shrugged and went over to the boys, where Kyle smiled and slid over to make room for her. "Not her!" Zero huffed. "That idiotic imbecile of a dragon will ruin everything!"

Alec gasped. Cierra looked up in surprise.

"Language," Kevin chided softly.

Kyle's reaction was nonverbal. He kicked Zero repeatedly in the shins while cursing through his teeth.

"Sor-ry," Zero muttered, rubbing his sore shins.

"It's okay, Kir," Kyle said warmly, "you can still help us."

Kirvam shook her head. "No. I'll go somewhere else."

Kirvam walked away from the pedestal and sat down next to Cierra, trying to study the notebook she held. It was a journal, bound in ancient, cracking leather and filled with yellowed parchment decorated with ink drawings and curving, graceful script.

"Uh, hey, Cierra," said Kirvam. "What're you reading?"

"The Dragon Guide," replied Cierra without looking up from the journal.

"Oh. How is a dusty old notebook going to help us defeat Kios?"

Cierra laughed drily. "This isn't just any notebook; it's a guide to all of the dragons native to Cypuric, showing their assets and their weaknesses."

"I have another question."

"Fire away."

"Alec said that I wasn't the only dragon to travel to Earth. If that's true, then where are the others?"

"I guess they're still out there."

"Am I supposed to find them?"

"D'you think you're alone in this?" Cierra cried, turning to face Kirvam. "We are the Dragon Keepers, and it's our job to protect all of Cypuric."

Kirvam nodded. "I understand now," she said softly.

As the Dragon Keepers discussed methods to defeat Kios, the sun slipped below the horizon, and everyone yawned and called it a night.

"Good luck," Kirvam said as she left to go to her bedroom.

"You too," Alec called down the corridor after her.

"Cierra," asked Kirvam as the two girls turned off their flashlights, "will I have to fight Kios alone?"

"'Course not," Cierra mumbled, "but just rest for now."

Kirvam sighed and closed her eyes, wishing that she had her normal life back.

CHAPTER EIGHT

Kirvam woke up before Cierra and crept into the room with the pedestal. Kevin, Alec, Zero, and Kyle were all conked out on the icy floor, snoring loudly. Barely breathing at all, Kirvam stepped up to the pedestal and whispered her command: "Show me Leo and Michaela Nielson."

Instantly the monitor flickered to life, showing a holographic image of a man and a woman standing in a kitchen.

"Mom! Dad!" Kirvam exclaimed softly, tears running down her cheeks.

"What are you doing?"

Kirvam whirled around and came face to face with Zero. "N-nothing," she stammered, switching off the monitor.

"Are you…crying?" asked Zero, the usual arrogance in his eyes melting away, only to be replaced with concern.

"No!" Kirvam shouted a little louder than necessary.

"Okay," replied Zero, turning to wake the others.

"Is everybody ready?" Kevin asked as soon as Cierra entered the room.

"Yes," chorused everyone.

"Very good. Alec and I will distribute the weapons."

Alec opened a large pack that lay on the floor next to him and pulled out a broad selection of swords, knives, and clubs. "Take your pick," Alec said. Zero chose a slender knife and a heavy wooden staff, Alec sheathed his ornate silver sword, and Kevin grabbed a pair of lethal-looking knives.

"No thanks," Cierra said, brandishing her set of igniting daggers.

"I'll pass too," said Kyle, unsheathing a sword that, like Cierra's daggers, burst into flames.

"What about me?" Kirvam questioned.

Zero rolled his eyes. "You don't need anything, doofus. You're a dragon. Does that ring a bell?"

"Oh," Kirvam replied lamely, "what can I do?"

"Seriously?" Zero groaned. "I'm really starting to doubt your abilities as a leader."

Kyle cocked an eyebrow. "Starting to?" he said teasingly.

Zero's face turned red. "I-I guess not," he mumbled, looking down at his feet.

"Anyway," said Alec, continuing where Zero had sort of left off, "in your Crystal Ice dragon form you have the ability to literally freeze your opponents in their tracks."

"How?"

"Just focus on Kios, and he'll be blasted to heaven and beyond," Kyle offered.

"So," said Kirvam slowly, "I have the power of immobility?"

"Pret-ty much."

"Alrighty then, let's get going!" Kevin said briskly. "Here's the plan: We go to the central peak in the Forever Mountains, attack whatever guards Kios has placed there, and storm into his lair for the final blow. Sound good?"

Everyone nodded in approval.

"Great! Time to go!"

This time the Dragon Keepers were more prepared. Each member carried a small leather satchel filled with necessities such as bread, cheese, an apple, a water bottle, and, for some, weapons. Cierra's bag also included the Dragon Guide, and Kyle's contained his MP3 player and earbuds, much to Zero's chagrin.

"I can't believe you're going to be listening to *music* while fighting Kios!" Zero complained loudly.

"Hey!" Kyle cried indignantly. "Don't harsh my mellow!"

Cierra shook her head in mock disapproval. "For shame, you guys! Fighting about petty things when we might die today!"

"Why is everyone so pessimistic?" Kyle moaned.

"My apologies," said Zero in a fake voice.

Soon the Dragon Keepers arrived at the foot of the main mount in the Forever Mountains. About three feet above their heads was a tarnished bronze plaque with a jumble of strange symbols etched into it.

"What does it say, Alec?" asked Cierra.

Alec shook his head. "I don't know. I think it's in the Ancient Dragon language, and only true dragons can read that."

"Kir could try," said Kyle.

Kirvam stepped up to the plaque and concentrated on its letters, which first came to her in the language Multa had used for her chant:

> "Uoy tsum raef tahw seil daeha,
> Siht yenruoj lliw eb lluf fo daerd.
> Raef eht sekans dna esu eht yek,
> Yrev, yrev ylsuoituac.
> Rehtag ruoy sdneirf dna evael eht nwot,
> Ot eht ssenkrad lla dnuora.
> Ereht uoy lliw dnif ya cigam rood,
> Kcolnu ti dna eh lliw eb on erom.

"Txen dnif eht ymene htiw eht ksam,
Uoy era gnimoc ot eht dne fo ruoy ksat.
Ekat noitaerc dna ekat noitcurtsed,
Dna uoy lliw evirra ta eht taerg noitcesretni.
Ekam ya esiw eciohc dna esoohc eht thgir htap,
Neht uoy rehpiced eht niap fo ruoy tsap.
Ekat siht egdelwonk uoy evah derehtag,
Dna eht ymene llahs eil detaefed, derehtiw.

Sey, uoy evah dehsinif ruoy dnarg erutnevda,
Won eraperp rof eht lavirra fo Retniw."

"Wow, Kirvam!" Kyle cried. "I think you're a natural!"

"Sure, Kyle," Zero said sarcastically, "but I think it's supposed to be in *English*."

"I'm *trying*," Kirvam snapped. Translating this language made her dizzy.

"You must fear what lies ahead,
This journey will be full of dread.
Fear the snakes and use the key,
Very, very cautiously.
Gather your friends and leave the town,
To the darkness all around.
There you will find a magic door,
Unlock it, and he will be no more.

"Next find the enemy with the mask,
You are coming to the end of your task.
Take creation and take destruction,
And you will arrive at the great intersection.

Make a wise choice and choose the right path,
Then you decipher the pain of your past.
Take this knowledge you have gathered,
And the enemy shall lie defeated, withered.

"Yes, you have finished your grand adventure,
Now prepare for the arrival of Winter."

Alec frowned. "This poem sounds oddly familiar."

"Yes it does," agreed Kevin. "'Winter' is the name Kios gave to his twisted dream for Cypuric."

"What is that?" Kirvam asked.

"The massacring of all the dragons that wouldn't join the Ragnauts," Kevin explained.

Kirvam shuddered. "They're kinda like Nazis."

"Uh, guys," Kyle said nervously, "I think I know who's guarding this place."

Everyone turned around right as a massive crack ran up the mountain.

CHAPTER NINE

Tons of rock and dirt crumbled away from the mountain, sending an avalanche of debris cascading down the slope.

"RUN!" Zero cried as a two-headed writhing, black, snake-like creature burst from the rock.

Cierra gasped. "It's the Morevan!"

Alec snapped his fingers. "I knew that rune looked familiar!"

"Grab your weapons!" Kevin cried.

Alec unsheathed his sword and charged at the Morevan, Kyle grabbed his sword too, and Zero activated his rocket boots and flew to one of the dragon's heads, knife in hand. Kevin pulled out his own knives, and Cierra did a backflip, landing squarely on the dragon's back with a dagger in each hand. Kirvam quickly transformed into a dragon and soared after Zero.

"So what exactly is the Morevan?" Kirvam called over the sound of metal on flesh and pained cries.

"Oh, it's just a Venos dragon with dark plasma poison that's capable of destroying everything in its path," Zero said, narrowly avoiding a stream of purple poison that was jetted his way.

"Dragon Godzilla!" Kyle added cheerfully as he ran past.

Suddenly realization dawned upon Kirvam. "Zero!" she cried.

"*I* am the key!"

Zero turned around. "Are you sure?"

Kirvam took a deep breath. "Yes."

"Okay." Zero nodded. "I'll distract the Morevan while you sneak up on Kios. His lair should be on the right side of the next mountain."

Kirvam darted away from the raging battle and ducked behind a pile of boulders. "Use the key," she whispered to herself.

All of a sudden the rocks behind her tumbled away, revealing a hidden entrance! Bracing herself for the worst, Kirvam took a tentative step into the dark corridor. Knee-deep in what she hoped wasn't bones and sewage, Kirvam trudged forward until she stumbled upon a wide-mouthed cavern. Stalactites and stalagmites surrounded the opening like jagged teeth in the mouth of some ferocious beast. Kirvam tried to steady her thundering heart and inched forward.

"Enter, Kirvam," a gravelly voice said, "I have been expecting you."

A dragon stood in the center of the bleak cavern. His dark purple eyes flashed fear into Kirvam; his muddy green-black scales seemed darker than the corridor Kirvam had just left. Wings of great size protruded from his back, gently opening and closing.

"Wh-who are you?" Kirvam stammered, trying to sound completely at ease.

"I have to say, Kirvam, you are a lot smarter than I expected," Kios said, abruptly changing the subject. "I must admit when I first heard of your arrival things were looking pret-ty grim for the Dragon Keepers."

Kirvam clenched her teeth. "How did you know I was here?"

Kios laughed coldly. "I have my ways."

"Well, I'm the Daughter of Agor, and I'm here to destroy you!" Kirvam cried. She started to concentrate on Kios's brawny form, hoping that a jet of ice would stab him through the heart.

"How noble of you, trying to be brave to impress your friends," Kios drawled, slinking around the edges of the cavern, "sadly, those pesky vermin will be disappointed upon learning the death of their precious leader. That is, assuming they survive."

"You take that back!" Kirvam roared. Rage and adrenaline

rushed through her body, and a stream of ice shot at Kios, slamming him into the stone wall.

"Why, you little…!" Kios snarled, lunging at Kirvam. His sharp claws sliced cleanly through her thigh, and golden blood spilled.

Kirvam desperately shot more ice at Kios, trying to ignore the throbbing pain in her leg, but he nimbly dodged each attack, ducking and rolling over the ground then retaliating with one of his own. Then Kios smashed his head into Kirvam's skull, and she fell to the ground.

"Foolish dragon," Kios chuckled, "you are nothing more than a hatchling."

"No." Just to speak made Kirvam's vision blur and her head spin.

Kios leaned down close to Kirvam. His breath reeked with the stench of death. "You should give up while you still can, new leader. You have failed."

I have *failed,* Kirvam thought despairingly. "You may have won the battle, but you haven't won the war," Kirvam whispered hoarsely.

Kios laughed once more. "I shall let you live, Daughter of Agor. After all, some of my Ragnauts have been needing training." He walked to the mouth of the cavern. "There is a traitor among you. Be wary."

Kirvam let her head fall to the floor. She watched Kios exit the cavern before closing her eyes in defeat. Hopefully, the Dragon Keepers could hold him back until she healed… With a final sigh, she reverted back to human form.

The sound of feet on stone thrummed in Kirvam's ears. She looked up in alarm only to meet eyes with Cierra.

"Kirvam! You're alright!" Cierra cried jubilantly.

Suddenly a wave of nausea hit Kirvam. She felt the back of her head, and her hand came away coated in blood.

"Are you okay?" Cierra questioned anxiously.

"Help," Kirvam moaned feebly, and everything went black once more.

"Kir!"

"C'mon, c'mon, wake up, wake up!"

"Hey, get some cloth from my pack and tear it into strips."

"What for?"

"Fresh bandages, you ding-dong!"

Kirvam slowly opened her eyes, but a massive headache made her close them again. The plethora of worried voices only increased her nausea.

"No, no, no, wake up!"

That was Zero's voice, sounding scared and concerned.

Kirvam forced herself to sit up, then took in her surroundings. She was back in the Dragon Keeper's cave, and they stood over her while Cierra dressed Kirvam's wound.

"Kirvam, listen to me," Alec said, "you need to get back into dragon form."

"Okay," Kirvam sighed, trying to ignore the throbbing pain in her skull. Bit by bit she transformed into a dragon and immediately felt the wound on her head start to close. "Why'd I have to turn into a dragon?" she asked.

"Because dragons are less susceptible to pain and they heal much faster than humans," Alec explained.

Kirvam winced as Cierra began to bandage the gash on her leg. "Did you guys beat Kios?"

Zero snorted. "A group of teenagers with absolutely no training taking down the strongest dragon? We never stood a chance."

"But," added Cierra, glaring at Zero, "we fought well for our abilities."

Kirvam cracked a smile. "So, all in all, you agreed with me."

Zero scowled.

Kirvam stood. The effort made her head throb again, but she refused to give in to pain. "Then what's the good news?"

"Whoever said there was good news?" Zero muttered.

Kyle cleared his throat. "Once you're completely healed, you can go to see your parents!"

Kirvam tried to blink back her tears.

"From there you can decide whether to continue this battle or to rejoin your parents," Alec said gently.

Kirvam took a deep breath. "I'll be ready."

CHAPTER ELEVEN

Three months after the battle in Cypuric, Leo Nielson stood at his kitchen window, gripping its sill until his knuckles turned white. He wasn't enjoying the lush scenery of his backyard; he was lost in thought. Just a little over three months ago he lost his only daughter, Kira, when she was taken by the Dragon Keepers. Even though Leo knew this was supposed to happen, he still wanted his little girl back!

"Leo?" a soft voice questioned. "Are you alright?"

Leo turned around and saw his wife standing in the kitchen doorway. "Michaela…" he murmured.

"Leo, I guess it was time. If they needed her, they needed her."

Leo whipped away from the window. "I don't care if they did! She was and still is a child, and she belongs with us!"

All of a sudden Michaela's face went white. "L-Leo!" she gasped, pointing at the window.

Michaela and Leo raced to the window right as a dragon stepped from a swirling mass of colors in their backyard. The dragon was a majestic being: shimmery, pearlescent scales, crystalline eyes, and large blue wings.

"Is that…?" Leo whispered in awe.

"Our daughter?" Michaela finished.

Then the doorbell rang.

Leo and Michaela bolted outside and swept their now-human daughter into their arms.

"Mom! Dad!" Kirvam cried.

Leo took a step back. "You look bigger than before."

"That's because I'm thirteen."

"Oh, Kira, welcome home!" Michaela exclaimed.

Kirvam looked away from her parents. "I go by Kirvam now, and I'm actually here to tell you something."

"That you're staying?" Leo suggested hopefully.

"No." Kirvam brushed away her tears. "I'm going to be staying in Cypuric with the Dragon Keepers."

"What?" Leo exploded. "I am your father, and I forbid you to do this!"

"You're not my real dad!" Kirvam snapped. "My father is a dragon."

Leo stopped yelling. "I…" he began.

Kirvam started to sob. "I'm sorry. Look, living here isn't who I am, no matter how much I love you."

"I guess this is goodbye," Leo choked.

"But you will visit us," Michaela instructed, wiping Kirvam's eyes.

Kirvam nodded. "Absolutely!"

Michaela and Leo Nielson embraced their foster daughter one more time and watched her walk through the portal.

"Goodbye," Leo whispered, and he and Michaela walked into their house.

Kirvam sat in the Dragon Keepers' headquarters, watching her holographic parents walk into their computer-generated house. She sighed and turned off the monitor, the image instantly dissolving into thin air.

"Hey."

Kirvam looked up and saw all of the Dragon Keepers standing around her. "What now?"

Alec spoke first. "Unfortunately, we just learned that Kios is still alive."

"Oh, joy," Kirvam groaned.

"And, as you know, the other leaders are still out there," Cierra continued.

Kyle stepped forward. "We need more people to help us."

"We can no longer fight this battle by ourselves," Zero added.

"What are you trying to tell me?" asked Kirvam.

Alec placed his hand on Kirvam's shoulder. "Kirvam," he said gravely, "are you prepared to tell the others?"